To: Joyce on her 5th Birt

May you always find your
comfy place !

2021 Mayu Kogh

Looking for My
Comfy Place

Written by Margie Krogh

Illustrated by Mary Barrows

RoseDog Books
PITTSBURGH, PENNSYLVANIA 15238

RoseDog Books
585 Alpha Drive
Suite 103
Pittsburgh, PA 15238
Visit our website at *www.rosedogbookstore.com*

ISBN: 978-1-6376-4714-1
eISBN: 978-1-6376-4754-7

Looking For My

Comfy Place

For all the comfy times with my kids,

Heather, Rob and Michelle as they were growing up

and now with all my grandchildren,

Elizabeth, Brian & Katherine,

Wyatt, Henry & Oscar and Isaac & Iris, who was

the one who actually inspired this little story!

I thank the Lord for each of you every day!

- All my love and hugs,
Mom and Gramma

I hop into bed and read my book until I get so sleepy

And when my eyes begin to droop, my nightly search begins...

Wiggling and Squiggling

Looking for my comfy place.

My sheets are too tight and bedspread too heavy.

I kick at the corners tucked in way too tightly and

throw back the covers to beat the heat... Fanning and Finicking...

Looking for my comfy place.

It seems so easy and should be so simple, but the right position can be so

unreachable. How about my side?... Okay, that's nice... but now where's my Teddy?

Here under my Little Pony or Raggedy Ann or one of my many other buddies?

Just Fussing and Fidgeting...

Looking for my comfy place.

Maybe my stomach would be softer to rest on... so rollover I go

sinking my head onto the pillow.

Oh!! It's too flat... I don't like that...

And my night light's way too bright... So I keep on...

Wiggling and Squiggling... and now—even Squinting...

Looking for my comfy place.

I think I'll try staring at the ceiling next.

Oh, fiddly sticks, my back is as flat as my pillow!

So onto my other side I roll, propping one leg up on top of the other.

No, that's way too straight... but wait, what's that?

It's my Teddy right down next to my toes. Right there, all the time under my nose so

unsuspecting and silent... but on I go...

Looking for my comfy place.

I know!! I will put one hand under my pillow and plop the other arm on top.

Sort of scoot in between my side and my tummy

with the covers pulled up around my neck.

There it is … that's it!

Could it get any better… than with my Teddy and me close together?

I think I could stay in this spot forever!

No more wiggling, squiggling, fussing or fidgeting!!

My spot is cozy, cushy and oh, so reassuring.

And just like that my search is over!

I'm finally done......

Looking for my comfy place.

Margie Krogh holds degrees in both Children's Ministry and Music from Wheaton College. She has a love and passion for both the Lord Jesus and children... not just her own children but the hundreds of others she has worked with throughout her lifetime as a Children's Ministry Director and piano teacher.

She grew up on a farm in Illinois but has lived in Penn Hills, Pa, a suburb of Pittsburgh for the last forty years. She and Bruce have been married for 45 years and are blessed with 3 adult children and their spouses and 8 grandchildren! Together, they all make her joy in life complete!

This is Margie's first children's book!

Mary Barrows is a freelance illustrator from a small town in Maryland. Since she was old enough to hold a crayon she has been drawing pictures of her favorite stories and she hasn't stopped yet. Her illustrations are done in a traditional style using ink, watercolor, gouache, colored pencil, graphite or whatever else she can get her hands on.

To contact email marybarrowsillustration@gmail.com